Ollie the Owllama

Kim Wilson

illustrated by Ashley Teets

Headline Kids
an imprint of Headline Books, Inc.
Terra Alta, WV

Ollie the Owllama

by Kim Wilson
illustrated by Ashley Teets

copyright ©2018 Kim Wilson

To order additional copies of this book, or for book publishing information, or to contact the author:

Headline Kids
P. O. Box 52
Terra Alta, WV 26764

Email: mybook@headlinebooks.com
www.headlinebooks.com

Ashley Teets—*Art Director*
Lucas Kelly—*Design/Layout*

Published by Headline Books
Headline Kids is an imprint of Headline Books

ISBN-13: 978-1-94-666435-8

Library of Congress Control Number: 2018944930

PRINTED IN THE UNITED STATES OF AMERICA

*To my llama-loving Lilly and owl-loving Emma,
my inspirations and creative partners in
bringing Ollie to life.*

*To my biggest fan and supporter, Jeff, thank you for
always believing in my dreams and in me.*

I love you all most.

Chapter 1

"Pah-hoo!" The llama spit and owl hoot flew out of Ollie the Owllama's* mouth all at once. This happened every time Ollie was upset.

*An owllama is part owl and part llama. Llamas spit when agitated or upset. Owls hoot. For Ollie, these traits put together produced a "Pah-hoo." This noise was often mistaken for a sneeze.

It happened when he did homework…when it rained…and even when he was served food he didn't like. He couldn't help it. The pah-hoo just came out!

This time his loud spit-hoot exploded as the meal of nettles and grass was served at school.

"Bless you!" exclaimed Miss Hildie, the llama day school lunch lady.

"Thank you, Miss Hildie," Ollie said with a sigh. He shook his head and grumbled to himself. "I did not sneeze. I just don't like eating nettles and grass."

"If you're not gonna eat that, can I have it?" his friend Stew asked.

"Help yourself."

Ollie spent the rest of lunchtime daydreaming about pancakes while his llama friends ate.

"Yum!" He woke himself as the loud exclamation came out of his mouth.

"Ring!" went the school bell. Lunch was over and Ollie's tummy growled.

Chapter 2

When Ollie got home that afternoon, his llama daddy noticed something was wrong. "Are you okay, buddy?"

"I spit with a hoot because I didn't like the food at lunch today," Ollie replied sadly. "And everyone thought I sneezed."

His daddy knew sometimes it was difficult for Ollie because he was different from all his owl and llama friends.

"Why don't you try and hold it in next time?" he suggested, trying to be helpful.

"I'll try." Ollie felt a little better. He was hopeful he could hold the pah-hoo in if he needed to.

Chapter 3

That evening, Ollie made his way across the field to the old barn. His tummy went, "Rumble! Grumble! Rumble!"

He could not wait until mealtime. But once he sat down at the long table with all his owl friends, he noticed the menu for the night was…

Mice… "Yuck!"

"How can you eat a mouse?" Ollie asked his friend Gwen.

"They are my favorite!" Gwen said as she popped one into her mouth.

Hold it in. Hold it in. Ollie said over and over in his head.

His cheeks puffed out as he held his breath. But his efforts made the spit-hoot burst out of his mouth even louder. "Paaaaah-hooooooo!"

All of the owl heads turned quickly toward him in surprise as the llama spit spewed across the table.

"Mind your manners, Ollie, and cover your mouth when you sneeze!" scolded Mr. Pepherhill, his owl night school teacher.

Embarrassed because everyone was staring at him, Ollie replied, "Yes, sir." But under his breath he said, "I did not sneeze. I just don't like eating mice."

Chapter 4

Ollie's mama was the smartest owl on the farm. He asked for her advice as soon as he got home from night school. "What can I do to stop pah-hooing, Mama? Everyone always thinks I'm sneezing."

The wise owl pondered for a moment. "Why don't you tell everyone it's not a sneeze? That it comes out when you're upset and you can't control it yet?" She paused. Then exclaimed in a matter-of-fact tone, "You are part llama and part owl. It makes perfect sense that you spit AND hoot. And sometimes it comes out all at once."

Ollie decided Mama was right. He would feel a lot better if everyone realized he wasn't sneezing.

With a rumbling of his still hungry tummy, he went to sleep. He dreamt all his friends turned into walking-talking pancakes. They looked and smelled delicious.

Just as Ollie was about to take a big bite out of Pancake Stew, he woke up with a jolt. The sun was beginning to rise when he realized, "It's Saturday!"

Chapter 5

Each Saturday morning the llamas woke up early and the owls went to sleep late. Everyone came together during this time for a big meal. They called it Brinner. It was Ollie's favorite meal of the whole week. All his friends and family were together… And there were usually pancakes! He had been looking forward to those golden, buttery pancakes. It made suffering through all the other meals of the week worth it. He was so hungry he could nearly taste the sweet syrup dripping down the fluffy stack.

As everyone sat down to eat, Mr. Pepherhill made an announcement over the loud speaker. "This Saturday we will be serving a very special dish. Grassy rodent casserole! Enjoy, everyone!"

"Yay!" everyone cheered, everyone but Ollie.

Chapter 6

"No pancakes?!" Ollie was disappointed and getting upset. The food made its way toward him. The smell of the grassy rodent casserole wafted to his nose. Before he even knew it was happening again, he let out a loud and uncontrollable,

"PAAAAH-HOOOOOOOOOOOOOOOOO!"

The table shook…forks went flying…drinks spilled…and droplets of spit went everywhere.

"Do you need a tissue, Ollie?" Gwen yelled from across the table in the chaos.

38

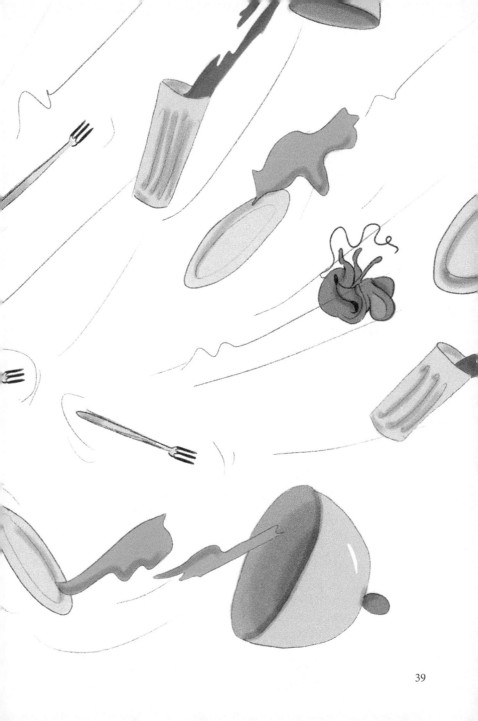

Ollie's llama neck stretched long and his owl feathers puffed out. He leaped onto the brinner table. "I DID NOT SNEEZE! I AM AN OWLLAMA! THAT MEANS SOMETIMES I SPIT WITH A HOOT!"

Everyone went silent, shocked by Ollie's outburst. "And I am so hungry for some yummy pancakes," he added quietly. He was quite flustered by the scene he had caused.

"Well, why didn't you just say so?" asked Gwen.

"Yeah," Stew chimed in.

"Pancakes it is!" exclaimed Miss Hildie. "Be back in a jiffy!"

Chapter 7

Ollie sat back down at the table. He was relieved everyone understood his pah-hoos were not sneezes.

A few minutes later a giant mountain of pancakes, drenched in melted butter and syrup, made it's way out of the kitchen toward Ollie.

So content after he scarfed down every last crumb, the only noise he made was a big loud, "BURP!"

"Ollie! Say excuse me!" his mother exclaimed.

Ollie smiled and said, "Sorry, Mama. Excuse me."

Llama FUN FACTS

- Llamas make good therapy animals; in general, they are calm, peaceful animals.

- The fibers in llama fur are fire-resistant.

- Llamas are social animals and like to stay in a herd.

- Llamas provide wool, and make great cart-pulling or pack animals.

- Llamas can be stubborn, especially when given too heavy a load. They will refuse to move and may even lie down until the load is lightened.

- Llamas belong to the camel family and can survive weeks without drinking water, instead gathering moisture from the food they eat.

- They typically only spit when they are agitated or provoked.

Owl FUN FACTS

- Owls can't move their eyes and must turn their heads to see things and they can turn their heads almost all the way around.

- The feathers that look like ears on an owl's head are called "ear tufts," but actually have nothing to do with hearing!

- Even though most owls are nocturnal, they have incredible vision both in the dark and the light.

- Owls are raptors, or birds of prey, and eat rodents, insects, fish, lizards, and more!

- Their keen sense of hearing allows them to hear even the slightest movements of their prey.

- After owls eat their prey, they spit up an "owl pellet" containing the bones and fur they are unable to digest.

- Owls communicate with hoots, but they also may screech or scream, whistle, or make facial expressions. They can be loud at times, but are able to fly almost silently.

Brinner [*Brin-er*] Noun—the combination of breakfast and dinner; an event that takes place soon after llamas wake and right before owls go to sleep; a time for all to get together and celebrate friendships…with pancakes, of course!

Chaos [*key-os*] Noun—a state of complete disorder and confusion.

Llama Day School [*Lah-muh Dey Skool*] Noun—where young llamas go to study the art of clearing fields and hauling loads; education given during the period of light after the sun rises and before it sets, when llamas are awake.

Nettle [*net-tle*] Noun—wild plant with leaves covered with fine hairs that sting when touched. *A llama food favorite.

Owllama [*Oul-lah-muh*] Noun—an animal with the soft wooly llama fleece and owl feathers, that spits and hoots, and stays up part of the day and part of the night.

Owl Night School [*Oul Nahyt Skool*] Noun—where young owls go to learn the skills needed to hunt; instruction provided during the period of darkness after the sun sets and before it rises, when owls are awake.

Pah-hoo! [*Pa-hoo*] Interjection—used to represent the noise an Owllama makes when they are upset; a combination of llama spit, "pah," and owl hoot, "hoo," together making quite a commotion! *Not to be confused with "Ah-choo!" which is clearly a sneeze.*

Scarfed [*skahrfd*] Verb—ate something quickly.

Vocabulary

Casserole [*kas-uh-rohl*] Noun—a mixture of foods cooked in a deep baking dish.

Content [*Kuhn-tent*] Adjective—satisfied with what one has.

Explode [*ik-splohd*] Verb—to burst with great force.

Flustered [*fluhs-terd*] Adjective—upset, unsettled, embarrassed; in a state of agitated confusion.

Grumbled [*gruhm-buhld*] Verb—complained in a low voice.

Jolt [*johlt*] Noun—a sudden movement.

Pondered [*pon-derd*] Verb—thought about something carefully.

Spewed [*spyood*] Verb—thrown out with great force or energy.

Uncontrollable [*uhn-kuhn-troh-luh-buhl*] Adjective— unable to be controlled or restrained.

Comprehension Questions

1. Was Ollie the Owllama fiction or non-fiction? How do you know?

2. Who was the main character?

3. How would you describe the main character? Why would you describe him or her that way?

4. What was the problem in the book? How was it solved?

5. What was your favorite part of the book? Why?

6. What was the MOST important event in the story? Why?

7. What did you learn from the book?

8. Did you hear the joke about the owl?

9. What is an owl's favorite dessert?

Answers 8: It was a real hoot! / 9: Miicecream

Growing up in upstate New York, Kim Wilson developed a love of reading and passion for writing at a young age. After graduating from SUNY Geneseo, where she studied writing, communication and public relations, she moved to Charlotte, North Carolina. It was there she had a career in marketing, married her husband Jeff, and is currently raising their two daughters, Lilly and Emma. The girls keep her days busy and her imagination active.

It was while Wilson and her daughters were playfully chatting that the furry and feathery Owllama was born. They were talking about their favorite animals and joked that it would be fun if the two were combined. A sketch-off ensued to find out what an Owllama would look like, and the initial vision of Ollie emerged. Following these playful brainstorming sessions, his character developed into the entertaining and likeable Ollie, complete with his characteristic signature, "Pah-hoo!" *Ollie the Owllama* is Wilson's first book. www.OllieTheOwllama.com.

Award-winning author and illustrator Ashley Teets holds a B.F.A in visual art with a minor in creative writing from Alderson Broaddus College. After two semesters of graduate work at West Virginia University she continued her graduate study through the Simmons College satellite graduate program at the Eric Carle Museum of Picture Book Art in Amherst, Massachusetts. She holds a Masters in Arts Administration through the University of Kentucky. Ashley is also a portrait artist, muralist and art instructor.

For more information visit
www.AshleyTeetsIllustration.com.